Doctor, Dolittle's
First Adventure

RED FOX READ ALONE

Red Fox Read Alones are fab first readers! With funny stories and cool illustrations, reading's never been so much fun!

Based on the stories by

HUGH LOFTING

Retold by Alison Sage

Doctor, Dolittle's First Adventure

Illustrated by Sarah Wimperis

RED FOX

A Red Fox Book

Published by Random House Children's Books
20 Vauxhall Bridge Road, London SW1V 2SA

A division of The Random House Group Ltd
London Melbourne Sydney Auckland
Johannesburg and agencies throughout the world

3 5 7 9 10 8 6 4 2

This Read Alone Novel first published in Great Britain
by Red Fox 2000

The Random House Group Limited Reg. No. 954009

www.randomhouse.co.uk

ISBN 0 09 940422 2

Printed and bound in Great Britain by Clays Ltd, St Ives PLC

Chapter One

Once upon a time, there was a doctor, and his name was John Dolittle. He lived in the little town of Puddleby-on-the-Marsh. Everyone liked him, especially the dogs and the cats and the children, who followed him wherever he went.

Doctor Dolittle had a white house with a big garden, and he lived there with his sister, Sarah Dolittle, who was good at organising things.

Sarah particularly liked organising money, and it made her cross that the doctor never had any. This was not because he was a bad doctor. He was brilliant at curing people. It was just that he could never see a sick animal without wanting to take it home and look after it.

He had goldfish in his pond, rabbits in the cupboard, white mice in the piano, and a hedgehog in the cellar.

There was a cow with a calf, and an old lame horse, as well as chickens and pigeons and two lambs and many other animals.

Doctor Dolittle loved all his pets, but perhaps his favourites were Dab-Dab the duck, Jip the dog, Gub-Gub the baby pig, Too-Too the owl, and the parrot, Polynesia.

All these animals cost a lot of money to keep. Worse still, the sick people did not like them. They did not want to share the waiting room with mice and squirrels.

One day, after a rich old lady sat on
the hedgehog and vowed never to visit
Doctor Dolittle again, his sister Sarah
said, 'John, how can you expect
patients to come and see you when you
keep all these animals in the house? We
are getting poorer every day. If you go
on like this, none of the best people
will have you for a doctor.'

'But I *like* animals better than the
"best people",' said the Doctor.

Soon, no one came to see him except the cats'-meat man and he only got ill once a year at Christmas. Then he would give the Doctor sixpence for a bottle of medicine. Sixpence a year was not enough to live on, even long ago, and soon Doctor Dolittle began to sell all his things so he could feed his animals. Even though he was poor, the dogs and cats and children still followed him through the town, just as they had done when he was rich.

Chapter Two

One day Doctor Dolittle was sitting in his kitchen talking to the cats'-meat man, who had a very good idea.

'Why don't you give up being a people's doctor and be an animal doctor?' he said. 'You know all about animals. You're brilliant with them. Anyone would think you *were* an animal, if you know what I mean. You'd make a lot more money looking after animals than people.'

When the cats'-meat man had gone, Polynesia the parrot flew down from the window to the Doctor. 'That man's got sense,' she said firmly. 'Be an animal doctor. Give up the silly people if they haven't brains enough to see that you're the best doctor in the world.'

'But there are lots of animal doctors already,' said the Doctor.

'Yes,' said Polynesia. 'But you would be the best. Listen to me. Did you know that animals can talk?'

'*You* can talk,' said Doctor Dolittle.

'Parrots are different,' said Polynesia proudly. 'We can talk in human language and bird language and lots of other languages as well. Now, if I say, "Polly wants a biscuit", you understand me. But what if I say, "*Ka-ka oi-ee fee-fee*"?'

The Doctor stared at Polynesia in surprise. 'I haven't any idea,' he said. 'What *does* it mean?'

'It means, "Is breakfast ready?" in bird language.'

The Doctor could hardly believe his ears. 'Why didn't you ever talk to me before like that?'

'Why should I?' said Polynesia. 'You wouldn't have understood.'

'Tell me more!' said the Doctor, his eyes shining with excitement as he grabbed a piece of paper and a pencil to write it all down. 'Let's start with the Birds' ABC. Don't go too fast!'

So that was how the Doctor began to learn the language of the animals. All that rainy afternoon, Polynesia sat on the kitchen table teaching him bird words.

At tea-time, Jip the dog came in. 'Look,' said Polynesia. 'He's talking to you.'

'But he's just scratching his ear,' said the Doctor.

'Animals don't only speak with their mouths,' said the parrot. 'They talk with their ears,  with their feet, with their tails – with everything. Sometimes they don't want to make a noise. See, Jip's twitching his nose.'

'What does that mean?' asked the Doctor.

'That means, "Do you know it's stopped raining?" Dogs nearly always use their noses for asking questions.'

It took a lot of patient work, but with Polynesia's help, the Doctor learned more and more about animals' language. Soon, he could talk to them himself and understand everything they said. Then he gave up being a people's doctor and started to cure animals instead.

One day, a horse was brought to see him. 'I'm going blind in one eye,' he said mournfully. 'That stupid vet over the hill – all he ever gives me is pills, and what I need is glasses.'

'Of course,' said the Doctor.

'Thank goodness I've found you,' said the horse. 'I wish my owner would realise it takes a much cleverer man to be a good animal doctor than a people's doctor.'

'Come back next week,' said the Doctor. 'I'll have the glasses ready for you.'

'What I'd really like,' said the old horse shyly, 'is a pair of sunglasses.'

The Doctor smiled. 'Certainly,' he said.

The horse began wearing his sunglasses. Thanks to the Doctor he stopped going blind.

It was the same with all the other animals. They told the Doctor what was wrong with them, and it was easy for him to cure them. News of this wonderful doctor spread like wildfire, and the big garden was always full of creatures waiting patiently to see him. He had special doors made so that every animal could wait with its own kind. He wrote HORSES over the front door, COWS over the side door, and SHEEP on the kitchen door. Even the mice had a tiny tunnel down in to the cellar.

Every living thing for miles around knew about Doctor Dolittle. Soon the birds carried news of him all over the world. Doctor Dolittle didn't care about being famous. He just went on curing sick animals and he was very happy.

Chapter Three

Sarah Dolittle was also very happy. So many people brought their sick animals to the doctor that soon there was lots of money. But the doctor was very soft-hearted and if sick animals needed to rest, he would let them sit in a chair on the lawn for as long as they liked. And if, when they were well again, they begged him to let them stay, he always said yes.

One day, Doctor Dolittle saw a man beating a poor little monkey on a string. He wanted it to dance for money. Doctor Dolittle was so angry he took the monkey from the man, gave him a  shilling and told him to go. The man was furious, but John Dolittle told him he would punch him on the nose if he didn't leave the monkey alone. The man shouted a lot of rude things but he went away and the monkey came to live with the Doctor. The other animals called him Chee-Chee, which means 'ginger' in monkey language.

Soon after this, the circus came to Puddleby. One of the crocodiles had terrible toothache and he escaped to see the doctor. Doctor Dolittle cured the toothache – but the crocodile liked it so much in the Doctor's house that when the men came from the circus to take him back, he begged the Doctor to let him stay. The Doctor hadn't the heart to turn him away. He let the crocodile sleep in the pond at the bottom of the garden, as long as he promised not to eat the goldfish.

It was not really the crocodile's fault that things started to go wrong. He was as gentle as a kitten. The problem was the humans. They were terrified that the crocodile would bite them and they thought he would eat their pets. They stopped coming to see the Doctor. Then Sarah Dolittle began to nag: 'John, no one is bringing us their pets any more. I won't stay in this house unless you send away that alligator.'

'It isn't an alligator,' said the Doctor. 'It's a crocodile.'

'I don't care what it is,' said his

sister. 'It's a nasty thing to find under the bed. And it eats the carpet. If you don't get rid of it, I'll go and get married! Then you'll be sorry.'

The Doctor saw there was no way out. 'All right,' he said. 'You'd better leave if you want to.'

So Sarah Dolittle went off and the Doctor began to look after everything himself.

The animals were happier than ever. But the Doctor became poorer and poorer. He didn't mind, but soon the animals themselves began to get worried. At last the owl, Too-Too, who was good at sums, worked out that there was only enough money to last for one more week. 'And that's if we have only one meal a day each,' he said.

Then Polynesia the parrot said, 'Let's help the Doctor. We animals can run the house ourselves. Perhaps we can find ways of saving money.'

They all started work straightaway. The monkey, Chee-Chee, did the cooking, Jip the dog swept the floors, Dab-Dab the duck did the dusting and made the beds, and Too-Too looked after the money. Gub-Gub the pig did the gardening and Polynesia, because she was the oldest, was in charge of everything.

They sold vegetables and flowers and home-made jam and the Doctor said that the house had never been run better. But they still did not have enough money. 'Never mind,' said the Doctor. 'We'll manage somehow.'

Chapter Four

That winter was terribly cold. One evening the animals were all sitting round the fire when the door flew open and Chee-Chee ran in, very upset.

'Doctor!' he cried. 'I've just had a message from Africa brought by a swallow. All my family and friends are dying from a terrible sickness. You are their last hope. You must go to Africa to help the monkeys!'

'Where is the swallow?' asked the Doctor. 'The swallows all flew south six weeks ago. She must be freezing cold!'

The swallow was brought in and put by the fire, and as soon as she warmed up a little, she repeated her story. 'And I will lead you back to Africa, if only you will come and help the poor monkeys.'

'Of course I'll help,' said Doctor Dolittle, looking worried. 'The only trouble is, how can we get to Africa?' He picked up his money box and shook it. There wasn't even a penny left. Chee-Chee looked as if he was about to burst into tears.

Then Doctor Dolittle said, 'Maybe we can borrow a boat. I once cured a sailor's baby and he told me that if there was anything he could do to help, I was just to let him know.'

Next morning, they went down to the sea and the sailor *did* remember the Doctor and agreed to lend him his boat.

The boat wasn't very big and the Doctor looked at all his animals and said, 'I am sorry but I have only got room for Jip the dog, Dab-Dab the duck, Gub-Gub the pig and the owl, Too-Too. I shall also take Chee-Chee, of course, and Polynesia and the crocodile, because Africa is their real home.'

At once the Doctor began arranging warm new homes for all the animals who weren't going to Africa. They said a very sad good-bye to him. 'I won't be long,' he promised.

Then he asked Polynesia's advice, because she knew all about sea travel.

'You need an anchor,' said Polynesia, 'That is very important, and you need plenty of food and plenty of rope.'

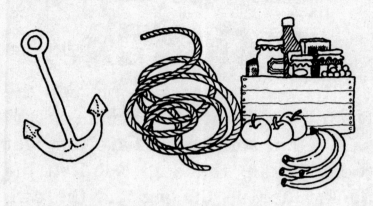

'But how shall we pay for it all?' moaned the Doctor. 'Never mind. I'll just have to ask everyone to wait for their money until we get back.'

Soon everything was ready and everyone went on board, terribly excited. Doctor Dolittle told Chee-Chee to pull up the new anchor and at last, they set sail for Africa.

Chapter Five

For six weeks they followed the swallow. As they sailed farther and farther south, it grew warmer and warmer. Polynesia, Chee-Chee and the crocodile enjoyed the hot sun. They couldn't wait to see Africa. Gub-Gub, Jip, and Too-Too the owl could only loll about in the shade, drinking lemonade.

Then one evening the sky grew dark and a great storm came up. Flashes of lightning crackled across the sky, and huge waves got so high they splashed right over the boat.

'We *must* reach land soon,' said the Doctor. Just as he spoke there was a terrible BANG. The ship stopped and rolled over on its side.

'We've hit a rock,' said Polynesia. 'And we're sinking fast.'

'We must have run into Africa,' said Doctor Dolittle. 'Never mind. At least we've arrived.'

'Abandon ship!' cried the parrot and everyone who could swim jumped into the water. Gub-Gub and Chee-Chee climbed to shore along a rope that Dab-Dab had tied to a palm tree, bringing the Doctor's baggage with them. The ship soon smashed to pieces on the rocks, but Doctor Dolittle and the animals scrambled safely on to the beach.

Next day, the sun was shining. 'Dear old Africa!' sighed Polynesia. 'It's good to get back. Just think, it'll be one hundred and sixty-nine years tomorrow since I was here! It hasn't

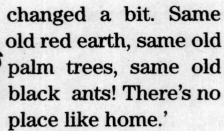

changed a bit. Same old red earth, same old palm trees, same old black ants! There's no place like home.'

Just then, Dab-Dab spotted the Doctor's hat, which had blown away in the storm, and she flew off over the waves to get it. She was surprised to find one of the white mice, very frightened, sitting inside it. 'I didn't want to be left behind,' squeaked the mouse. 'So I hid on board. When the storm came, I thought I was going to be drowned. Then the Doctor's hat floated by and I got into it.'

'A stowaway!' said Polynesia, when the white mouse had been brought to shore.

They were all talking at once when a man came towards them out of the forest. 'This is the land of the Jolliginki,' he said sternly. 'I have been sent to take you to my King. Follow me.'

'We'd better do as he says,' said the Doctor peacefully, and he picked up his luggage and set off, followed by all the animals.

Chapter Six

They had not gone far when they reached the palace where the King lived with his Queen, Ermintrude, and their son, Prince Bumpo. The King was sitting outside under an umbrella with Queen Ermintrude.

He was frowning and when he saw the Doctor he said, 'Once I was very kind to a stranger, but he stole my gold and killed my elephants for their ivory tusks. I swore that no one should ever travel through my country again.' He waved his hand. 'Take this man away to prison. At once!'

Six soldiers stepped forward and led the Doctor and the animals away and locked them up in a stone dungeon with only one tiny window.

Then Gub-Gub the pig began to cry, and Chee-Chee told him to keep quiet.

'Shh,' said the Doctor. 'Are we all here?'

'Polynesia's escaped,' grumbled the crocodile. 'Typical bird, sneaked off and left her friends.'

'No, I didn't!' said an indignant voice and the parrot climbed out of the Doctor's pocket. 'I had to hide, otherwise they would have shut me in a cage. I've got a plan to save us.'

As soon as it was dark, Polynesia

flew through the bars of the prison
to the palace. There was a broken
window in the palace kitchen and she
crept through it and flew up to the
King's bedroom. The Queen had gone
out to a dance and the King was fast
asleep. Polynesia crept in and got
under the bed. Then she coughed just
like Doctor Dolittle.

'Mmm?' said the King. 'Whassat,
dear?' He thought it was the Queen,
back from the dance.

Then Polynesia coughed again, even
louder.

'W-who's that?' said the King, now
wide awake.

'I am Doctor Dolittle,' said the parrot proudly.

'What are you doing in my bedroom?' asked the King angrily. 'How did you get out of prison?'

Then the parrot laughed, a long, jolly laugh, just like the Doctor's.

'Stop that!' ordered the King. 'Where are you?'

'Foolish King,' said Polynesia gravely. 'Don't you realise who I am? I am the great John Dolittle, and I have made myself invisible. There is nothing I cannot do. Now listen. If you do not let me and my animals out of prison, I will make you and all your people sick, just like the monkeys. If you have not freed us by dawn tomorrow, you will all be very sick.'

The King was terrified. 'Oh, your excellency! I had no idea. It shall be as you say. Don't hurt us, please!' And he jumped out of bed and ran to tell his soldiers to set the Doctor free.

As soon as he had gone, Polynesia flew out of the broken window, back to the Doctor. It was a pity that just at that moment the Queen came back from her dance. She saw Polynesia and told the King, who realised that he had been tricked. With a roar of rage he ran down to the prison, but the door stood open. The Doctor and all his animals had escaped.

Chapter Seven

Then the King fell into a terrible rage. He ordered everybody into the jungle to catch the Doctor. 'And don't come back until you have found him!' he yelled.

Luckily, Chee-Chee knew the way through the jungle and after a few hours of hurrying along the thick leafy paths he said proudly, 'I think we have given them the slip.'

But the smaller animals were very tired and soon Gub-Gub the pig started to cry. Polynesia gave him some coconut milk, which he liked tremendously. She and Chee-Chee found all kinds of delicious things to eat: dates and figs and peanuts and yams. They made a wonderful drink out of wild honey and oranges. At night, everyone slept on piles of dried grass, and even Gub-Gub began to enjoy their trip very much.

But the Doctor was getting worried, because every day's delay meant more sick monkeys. He would have been even more worried if he had known that the King's men were still following them. And they were getting closer every day.

One evening, Doctor Dolittle and the animals came upon a group of monkeys, led by Chee-Chee's cousin, waiting to welcome them. When the monkeys saw the Doctor had arrived, they gave a big cheer and waved. But the King's men had also heard the cheering and they came racing after them. Suddenly there was pandemonium. Everyone was running, shouting, tripping and panicking.

'Quick!' cried Chee-Chee. Doctor Dolittle and his friends followed him, and there in front of them was the

Land of the Monkeys. But they couldn't reach it because there was a steep cliff and a river in the way. They were trapped!

'Don't panic,' said Chee-Chee's cousin. 'We'll make a bridge!' Even the Doctor wondered how they were going to do that without any rope. Then all of a sudden he saw that the monkeys were making a bridge *out of themselves*, just by holding hands and feet.

'Hurry!' cried Chee-Chee's cousin. 'Walk over! All of you!' One by one, they scampered over the living bridge.

John Dolittle was the last to cross, and just as he reached the other side, the King's men came running up to the edge of the cliff. They shook their fists and yelled with rage to see the Doctor escaping again, but there was nothing they could do.

Chee-Chee smiled at the Doctor. 'Many great explorers would give years of their lives to see what you have just seen,' he said. 'You are the first person ever to see the famous Bridge of Apes.'

The Doctor felt very pleased.

Chapter Eight

Doctor Dolittle was now very busy. There were thousands of sick monkeys. Many had already died.

The first thing he did was to separate the sick monkeys from the well ones. Then he asked the well monkeys to build a huge house with lots of beds in it. This was going to be the hospital. But so many of the monkeys were ill, there were not enough well ones to do the nursing. So he sent messages to all the other animals, asking for help.

The Leader of the Lions was the first to answer. 'What *me*? Look after a lot of dirty monkeys? Why, I wouldn't even eat them between meals!'

'I didn't ask you to eat them,' said the Doctor, quietly. 'Just to nurse them. Listen, one day you may be in trouble yourself. Then you'll need help, too.'

'Lions are never *in* trouble,' smirked the Leader of the Lions. 'They only *make* trouble.' And he stalked off into the jungle.

Doctor Dolittle was at his wits' end. How was he going to nurse all the sick monkeys?

But when he got back to his den, the Leader of the Lions discovered that one of his little cubs was sick too. The Queen Lioness was terribly worried and said to her husband, 'Go to that Doctor at once. Tell him you're sorry and that the lions will do anything he asks. Then maybe he will cure our son.'

So the Leader of the Lions went back to the Doctor and said, 'Er – would you mind looking at our cub? He doesn't look too well. And of course, we lions will help you look after the monkeys. Only I won't wash them, you understand. The other animals will have to do that.'

Then the Doctor was very happy. He cured the little cub, and all the animals – the leopards and the antelopes and the giraffes and the zebras – came to help him with the monkeys. He soon had more nurses than he needed.

At the end of the first week, the monkeys began to get better, and by the end of the second week, the big house full of beds was empty. Soon the last monkey was well, and the Doctor's work was done. He was so tired he went to bed and slept for three whole days and nights.

While he was asleep, the monkeys held a council. 'What shall we give the Doctor as a present for helping us?' they asked.

'Bananas!' said one.
'Coconuts!' said another.
'A new house!' said a third.
'No,' said Chee-Chee. 'The Doctor must go home to Puddleby. He can't take much with him. But I know what he *would* like.'
'What's that?' asked the monkeys.
'The Doctor likes animals,' said Chee-Chee. 'If you can persuade a really rare creature to go with him, he would love that.'

Then all the animals thought hard.

'What about an iguana?'

'Not rare enough,' said Chee-Chee.

'An okapi?'

'They are nice, but they aren't very rare.'

'Then what about a pushmi-pullyu?' said a little red spider monkey.

'The Doctor has never even heard of a pushmi-pullyu,' said Chee-Chee. 'That would be perfect.'

Chapter Nine

Pushmi-pullyus are very rare. In fact, no one knows if there are any left at all today. They have no tail, but a head at each end and sharp horns on each head. They are very shy and very hard to catch since only one half of the pushmi-pullyu sleeps at a time and the other head is always awake – and watching. They live in the deepest, darkest part of the forest and it is said that they are related to the last of the unicorns.

The monkeys hunted patiently through the forest. Then one monkey spotted some very odd-looking hoof prints and guessed that the pushmi-pullyu was hiding in the long grass by the river. The monkeys joined hands and made a circle round the long grass. The pushmi-pullyu tried to break through but couldn't, and in the end he sat down and asked the monkeys what they wanted.

'Will you go to Puddleby with Doctor Dolittle?' asked the monkeys.

'Never!' said the pushmi-pullyu, shaking both his heads hard.

Then the monkeys explained to him how kind the Doctor was, and how good he had been to all the animals.

The pushmi-pullyu still shook his heads. 'No! I'm much too shy.'

For three days the monkeys tried to persuade him. In the end, the pushmi-pullyu said he would come and meet the Doctor. 'But I'm not promising anything,' he said.

Soon Chee-Chee was knocking on the door of Doctor Dolittle's hut.

'We've brought you a pushmi-pullyu,' he said proudly. 'It's the only two-headed creature in the world. When you take him home, you will be famous. You'll soon have lots of money.'

'But I don't want money,' said the Doctor.

'Yes you do,' said Dab-Dab the duck. 'We've got to pay back all the people we borrowed from, remember? And what about the sailor's boat?'

But the Doctor wasn't listening. He was smiling at the pushmi-pullyu. 'Do you want to come with us?' he asked kindly.

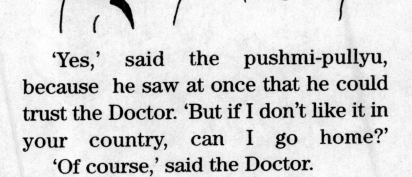

'Yes,' said the pushmi-pullyu, because he saw at once that he could trust the Doctor. 'But if I don't like it in your country, can I go home?'

'Of course,' said the Doctor.

Soon it was time to leave and the monkeys gave the Doctor a farewell party. Many animals came, and there were mangoes and pineapples and honey and all kinds of good things to eat.

The Doctor stood up and said, 'Dear friends. I am not good at long speeches, but I do want to say how sad I am to leave you all. I won't forget you. Remember not to let flies sit on your food. And, er, I'm sure you will always be happy.'

He sat down and all the animals clapped and shouted until they had no voices left.

Next day, every single monkey wanted to say good-bye and it was late in the afternoon before the Doctor was able to set off.

'Be careful!' warned the monkeys. 'The King of the Jolliginki is still angry about the trick you played on him.'

'Mmm,' said the Doctor. 'What really worries me is where we'll get a new boat from. Never mind. Perhaps we'll find one. No use crossing your bridges before you come to them.'

Chapter Ten

The Doctor and his animals travelled through the forest for several days and everyone grew tired and thirsty. 'Chee-Chee,' begged Gub-Gub. 'Do get some coconut milk. Please!'

But when Chee-Chee came back with the coconuts, there was no sign of the Doctor or any of the animals. Hot and bothered because Gub-Gub kept wandering off after ginger roots, Polynesia had taken the wrong turn and they were now completely lost.

They walked round and round in circles until they found themselves in the back garden of the palace of the King of Jolliginki. At once, the King's soldiers grabbed them. All except Polynesia who flew away before the soldiers could capture her.

'Ha!' said the King. 'You won't escape this time. Put double locks on the prison doors! You will scrub my kitchen floors for the rest of your lives.'

Too-Too the owl, Dab-Dab the duck, the white mouse, the crocodile, Jip the dog and the pushmi-pullyu all tried to look for some way out of their prison.

There was none. Gub-Gub began to sniff noisily. 'Don't cry,' said the Doctor. 'Polynesia has escaped. She'll think of something.'

Polynesia was sitting in a tree in the palace garden, blinking her eyes. This was always the sign that she was thinking extra hard. All at once she saw Chee-Chee, swinging through the trees. He was still looking for the Doctor.

'Where have you been?' said Chee-Chee crossly.

Polynesia explained what had happened. Chee-Chee was very angry. 'The King's palace of all places! Don't you know your way?'

'It's all Gub-Gub's fault,' said Polynesia. 'I went the wrong way. But shh! Here comes the Prince!'

Prince Bumpo came wandering along the path and sat down on the bench beneath the tree where Polynesia and Chee-Chee were hiding. He opened a book.

Polynesia's eyes gleamed. She'd had an idea.

She flew down with a little twig in her beak and perched just above Bumpo's head. Then she began waving the twig backwards and forwards in front of him. She made a low humming sound in her throat.

Prince Bumpo watched the twig moving to and fro and his eyes began to close.

'Can you hear me, Prince?' said Polynesia softly.

'Yes,' said the Prince in a dull, flat sort of voice.

'Bumpo, there is something important you must do.'

'There is something important I must do,' said Bumpo in the same flat voice. His eyes were tight shut.

'In your father's prison is a very great man.'

'A very great man,' agreed Bumpo.

'You must find a ship and set him and all his animals free.'

'I must find a ship and set him free,' repeated Bumpo.

'Go! At once! And tell no one!' said Polynesia.

'At once. Tell no one,' said Bumpo. He got to his feet and set off for the palace. He looked as if he was sleepwalking.

'What's the matter with him?' said Chee-Chee. 'Is he really going to set the Doctor free?'

'I hope so,' said Polynesia. 'He's hypnotised,' she explained. 'Many years ago I belonged to a magician and he taught me how to do that.'

They hurried to the prison and told Doctor Dolittle to get ready to escape. Some time later, the Prince arrived with a heavy bunch of keys.

'I have found a ship and I will set you free,' said the Prince in the same wooden voice.

'Good,' said Polynesia. 'And you will remember nothing about what has happened.'

'Nothing,' agreed the Prince. He leaned against the wall of the empty prison, smiling after them happily.

The animals ran through the forest to the beach, where the ship was waiting. 'How shall we find our way back home?' asked Dab-Dab. As she spoke there was a great rustling of wings. It was the swallows, returning to the North for the summer.

'We'll follow the swallows,' said the Doctor.

The moon shone on the water as they lifted anchor and set sail. Only now everyone became very sad. Chee-Chee, Polynesia and the crocodile had decided to stay behind in Africa because it was their home.

The Doctor promised to come and visit them, but they still climbed on to the rocks crying bitterly and waving until the ship was out of sight.

Chapter Eleven

The weather was good and soon the Doctor was well on the way home. Then one bright morning, Dab-Dab saw a red sail a long way behind them.

'I don't like the look of that sail,' she said.

Jip the dog was snoozing on deck. All at once he began growling in his sleep. 'I smell trouble,' he snarled. 'Six bad, evil men.' Then he barked loudly and woke up.

'What's the matter, Jip?' asked the Doctor.

'It's that boat,' said Jip. 'I smell something very bad about it.'

'It's chasing us,' whimpered Gub-Gub.

And it was. It had three red sails, and it was getting nearer every minute.

'They must be pirates!' whispered Dab-Dab nervously. 'Run downstairs,  Jip, and bring up more sails,' said the Doctor. 'We must try and go faster.' But even with all the sails they could find, the pirate ship was still getting closer and closer.

'This is a stupid boat,' whined Gub-Gub. 'I bet Prince Bumpo found the worst one in the whole of Africa.'

'We'll have to hide,' decided the Doctor. 'But where?'

'There's a little island over to the left,' said one of the swallows who had flown down to see what was the matter.

As fast as they could, the Doctor and the animals steered for a very pretty island with lots of sandy beaches and a big green mountain in the middle. The swallows guided them into a little bay which could not be seen from the open sea.

The animals were delighted to stretch their legs again. They galloped on to the white sand, squealing with joy. Just as he was getting off the ship, the Doctor noticed a stream of rats running down the gangplank. One big rat came forward as if he wanted to talk to the Doctor. Jip ran after him, barking. He loved chasing rats.

'Stop it, Jip,' said the Doctor. 'Is anything the matter?' he asked the rat, kindly.

The rat looked nervous. 'Er – Doctor. You know that rats live in ships, don't you?'

'Of course,' said the Doctor.

'And you know that rats always leave when a ship is going to sink?'

'I've heard people say that,' agreed the Doctor. 'A good idea, I've always thought.'

'Have you?' said the rat, eagerly. 'You don't think it's – you know – cowardly?'

'Not at all,' said the Doctor. 'So you are trying to tell me–'

'Your ship is going to sink in a few hours. I know it. I've got a tingling feeling in the tip of my tail, and it's never wrong. It's a bad ship. Don't sail in it anymore. Good-bye.' And with that, the rat scurried off on to the beach after his friends.

'Thank you for warning us!' called the Doctor. 'That was very lucky. We could all have been drowned. Now we'll have to explore the island.'

The animals loved the cool green grass, especially the pushmi-pullyu, who was very bored with the dried apples he had been eating on board ship.

They hadn't gone far, when two swallows flew down, very excited.

'Those pirates!' they twittered. 'They've found your ship! They're going on board now to steal your things. Why don't you get on *their* ship and sail away?'

'What a good idea!' said the Doctor.

They all ran back to the beach and there was the ship with red sails. It looked quite empty.

One by one, the animals sneaked on board. They lifted the anchor without a sound, and began moving out of the bay. Then suddenly, Gub-Gub sneezed so loudly the pirates on the other ship rushed up on deck to see what the noise was.

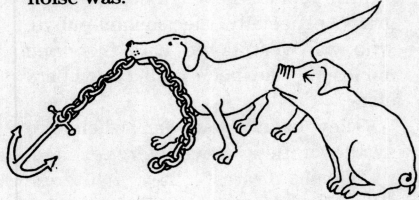

When they saw that the Doctor was escaping, they sailed the other boat across the mouth of the bay. Now the Doctor and the animals were trapped.

Then the pirate chief started laughing. 'You thought you could trick ME, the Barbary Dragon. But you failed. Now I am going to have that pig and that duck of  yours. We'll have pork chops and roast duck for supper tonight. And your friends are going to have to send me a sack full óf gold before I let you go. *If* I let you go, that is!'

Gub-Gub began to cry and Dab-Dab got ready to fly for her life. Too-Too whispered to the Doctor. 'Keep him talking. Our old ship is going to sink very soon, the rats said so.'

'I can't keep talking for hours,' said the Doctor.

'Don't bother,' growled Jip, showing his teeth. 'Let's fight!'

'It's all right for you,' squealed Gub-Gub. 'They're not going to eat *you*.'

The pushmi-pullyu said nothing. He had already started to sharpen his horns on the mast, getting ready for a fight.

The pirates sailed closer. 'Got any apple sauce?' they jeered. The animals waited grimly. All of a sudden, the pirates stopped laughing. They were staring at their feet. They were tipping sideways!

'What's going on?' yelled the Dragon. 'The boat's leaking, you great weevil brain!' barked Jip. Of course the Dragon couldn't understand, but he could see that the ship was sinking.

Faster and faster the boat dipped in the water and the pirates were now desperately climbing up the mast to stay dry. Then with a horrible gurgle, the ship sank to the bottom of the sea. The six pirates were left bobbing around in the deep water of the bay.

'Swim to our ship, men!' shouted the Dragon. But then the water started to froth and boil. All over the bay, triangular fins were arrowing in on the pirates.

'Sharks!' screamed the pirates.

The sharks ignored the pirates and swam over to the Doctor.

'Greetings, Doctor,' said the biggest shark. 'We know these pirates. They are an evil lot. Do you want us to eat them?'

'No,' said the Doctor. 'But could you get that one called the Dragon to swim over here?' So the shark went and chased the Dragon over to the Doctor.

'Listen, Dragon,' said the Doctor sternly. 'You have killed a lot of people and these sharks want to eat you. But I'm going to give you one more chance.'

'What is it?' squeaked the pirate, looking sideways at the big shark who was smelling his leg under water.

'You must promise to give up being a pirate. You must never even go to sea again.'

'But what shall I do?' wailed the Dragon.

'You and all your men can stay on
this island and grow bird-seed for
the canaries that live here,'
said the Doctor.

'Can't I even be
a sailor?' groaned
the pirate.

'No,' said the Doctor. 'You can't.'

'Bird-seed! *Me*!' muttered the
Dragon. Then he looked down and saw
that the shark was smelling his other
leg. 'All right,' he said sadly. 'We'll grow
bird-seed.'

'Don't forget,' said the Doctor. 'If
you break your promise, I shall get to
hear about it.'

Then the sharks let the pirates swim
ashore, and the Doctor and the animals
set sail once more for Puddleby.

Chapter Twelve

The next day, the animals went wild with excitement over their new ship.

'It's gorgeous,' sighed Dab-Dab. 'Primrose silk sheets, silver dishes and all sorts of wonderful things to eat and drink.'

There was also a small locked door with no key, and everyone was anxious to know what was behind it.

'Shh!' said the owl, Too-Too. 'There's someone in there!'

'I can't hear anything,' said Dab-Dab

'He's trying not to cry,' said Too-Too.

'How do you know?' asked Gub-Gub.

'Because I heard a tear drop fall on his sleeve,' said Too-Too.

'Well, that settles it,' said the Doctor. 'We must knock down the door as fast as we can.'

Doctor Dolittle chopped a big hole in the door with an axe, but it was so dark in the room that at first he couldn't see a thing. When he struck a match, he saw a boy sitting on the floor. The boy jumped to his feet and shouted, 'Are you a pirate?'

Doctor Dolittle stared and then he laughed. 'Do I look like a pirate? I'm a doctor.'

The boy grinned and said eagerly, 'Then where's my uncle?'

'I don't know anything about your uncle,' said the Doctor. 'Let's have some tea and then you can tell us what happened.'

'We were out fishing and the pirates came and sank our boat,' said the boy. 'Then they tried to make my uncle be a pirate too. He's a wonderful sailor, you see. But he wouldn't. So they got angry and there was a fight.' The boy's eyes filled with tears. 'I don't know what happened then because they shut me in here. Maybe they threw him in the sea.'

The Doctor looked serious. 'What does he look like?'

'He's got red hair,' said the boy, 'and an anchor tattoo on his arm. His boat is called the *Saucy Sally*.'

Dab-Dab whispered in the doctor's ear, 'Why don't you ask the porpoises? They know everything that happens in the sea.'

'Good idea,' said the Doctor.

The boy stared at him. 'Did you make those funny clicking noises?' he asked.

The Doctor smiled. 'I was talking to Dab-Dab in duck language,' he said.

'I never knew ducks had a language,' said the boy. 'And what is that funny-looking animal with two heads?'

'Shh!' whispered the Doctor. 'That's the pushmi-pullyu. He's very shy.'

Chapter Thirteen

The Doctor left the boy down below with the animals and went on deck to look for passing porpoises. Soon a whole school came by, and he asked if they had seen the boy's uncle.

'He's not dead,' said the porpoises. 'We've seen his boat at the bottom of the sea, but we haven't seen *him*.'

'Good,' said the Doctor. 'Now for the eagles!'

He called up six different kinds of eagle and they soared majestically to the east, south, north and west. At last they returned.

'We have searched all the seas, and all of the islands and the cities in this half of the world. He is not to be seen,' they said. 'Alive or dead.'

'If you ask me,' said Jip, 'we need someone who knows what they're doing.'

'Like who?' said Dab-Dab.

'Like *me*,' said Jip proudly. 'Ask the boy if he has anything belonging to his uncle.'

At once the boy brought out his uncle's handkerchief. Jip sniffed hard. 'Cough drops!' he snorted. 'Any dog can sniff out cough drops from a hundred miles.'

'Can they really?' said the Doctor, very impressed.

For two days, Jip tried the north, east, and south winds. But there was not a sniff of cough drops. Then on the third day he woke the Doctor before it was light. 'I've got it!' he barked. 'Cough drops! On the west wind.'

The boy was so happy he almost cried and they sailed as fast as they could to the west. Soon they could see a great black rock sticking out of the sea.

'Over there!' barked Jip.

'Don't be silly,' squealed Gub-Gub. 'There's no one there.'

'Listen, you chunk of warm bacon,' growled Jip. 'He *is* there. I can smell him.'

Jip was right. The boy's uncle was asleep in a little cave in the rock, where the pirates had marooned him. He had nothing to eat except his cough drops.

The Doctor took the boy and his uncle back to their home and then he and the animals sailed on for Puddleby.

It was midsummer when they returned home at last. All the animals they had left behind were very happy to see them again. The Doctor gave the pirate boat to the sailor. And Chee-Chee was right. Doctor Dolittle did become famous. Everyone wanted to hear about the pushmi-pullyu, and Doctor Dolittle soon had enough money to pay everyone back. He even had some to spare.

'It's good not to have to worry,' he said to Dab-Dab.

'It certainly is!' said Dab-Dab who was toasting muffins for tea.

Far away in Africa, the monkeys were chattering to each other. 'I wonder what Doctor Dolittle's doing now. Do you think he'll ever come back?'

'I hope he will!' squeaked Polynesia.

'I'm sure he will,' said the crocodile from the black mud of the river. 'He'll be back for more adventures. Now go to sleep!'